# A Home for *Wingtip!*

# This Bookatilly book belongs to

_____

# A Home for Wingtip!

Autographed by Wingtip

Story by Linda G. Shane
Illustrated by Kaylyn Urban

Bookatilly Books™

Copyright
© 2016 Linda G. Shane
All rights reserved.

No part of this publication may be reproduced, stored in a retrieval system, transmitted in any form or by any means, electronic, mechanical, photocopy, recording, or any other – except for brief quotations in printed reviews, without prior permission from the publisher.

ISBN: 978-0-9978025-0-4
Library of Congress Control Number: 2016913562

www.facebook.com/LindaGShane
www.lindagshane.com

First US Edition 2016
Printed in the USA

Bookatilly Books
PO Box 2324
Hayden ID 83835

**BOOKATILLY BOOKS™**

HAYDEN, IDAHO

bookatillybooks@gmail.com

*To my 12 grandchildren – you are loved.*

In the city of Shoestring lived a shoe named Wingtip.
He had a twin brother named Sole; their owner's name was Arch.
Sole fit on Arch's left foot, and Wingtip was always on his right.

At the end of their laces were aglets, who never said a word. The shoes had great journeys together with Arch: whether they went to sporting events, shopping, dining...

or just relaxing by a fire. They were always delighted for new adventures and giving Arch support to aid his feet.

One day, something terrible happened! Arch put Wingtip and Sole in his gym bag. As Arch got out of his truck, Sole fell out of the bag.

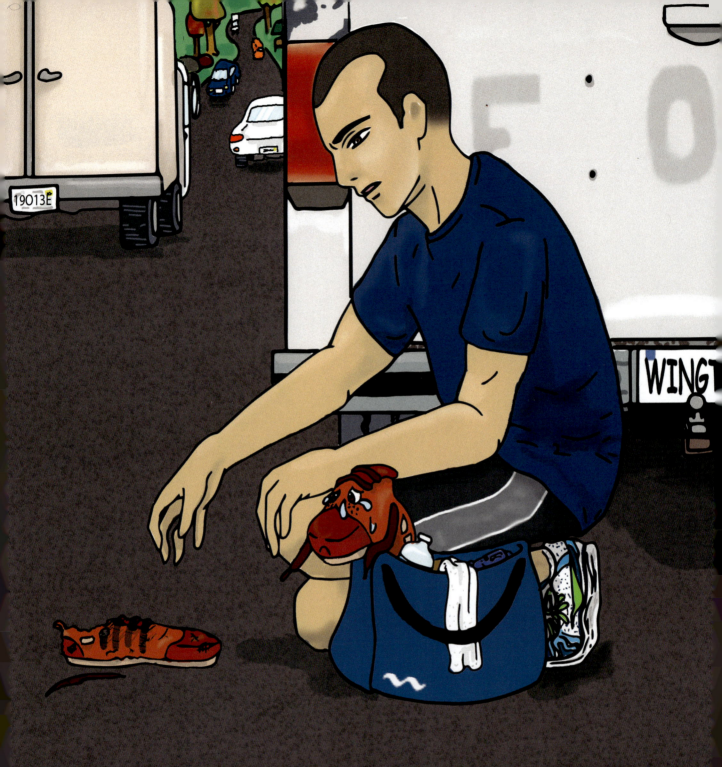

When Arch discovered that Sole was missing, he searched all over, finding Sole completely ruined, because a truck had run over him!

Wingtip cried, and when Arch picked up Sole, he too, felt the loss. He loved his shoes, but he knew he could never find another match for Wingtip.

Sadly, Arch laid Wingtip and Sole in the trash and drove away.

Sorrowful, Wingtip said, "I have lost my brother. What good am I, since man has two feet and needs right and left shoes?"

Just then, a dog wandered by and saw Wingtip.
He grabbed Wingtip and played with him. Wingtip was
happy to make a new friend! However, the dog got tired of him,
and dropped Wingtip by a dumpster.

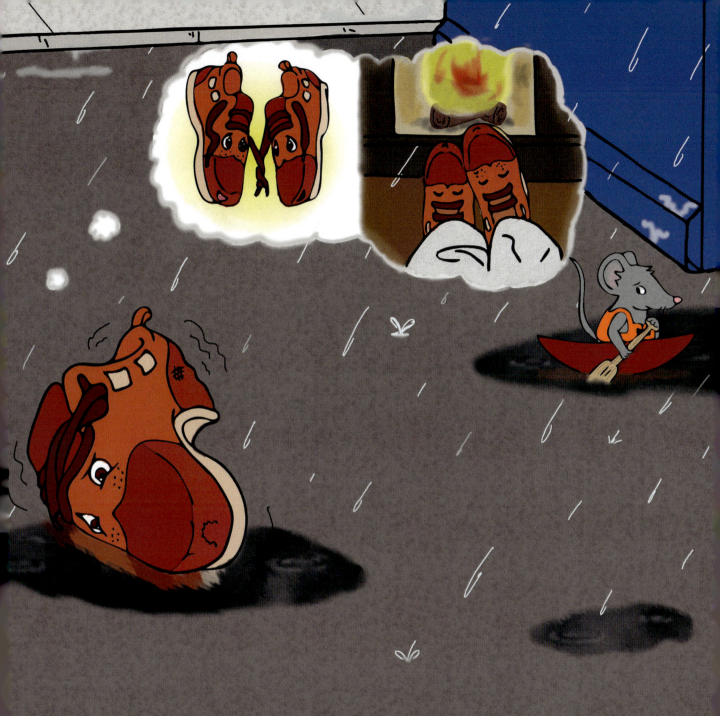

That night a heavy rain came, and Wingtip got soaked and cold. He lay there shivering, missing his brother and the comfort of his owner's foot and warm home.

"Not even a dog wants just one shoe," he said sadly.

The next day, the hot sun warmed him and dried him out too much, making him older looking. His tongue hung out from the heat.

To add to his misery, the garbage inside the dumpster called Wingtip mean names and asked, "How come an old, worn-out shoe like you isn't in here with us? You are garbage, too!"

Wingtip said nothing, but their hurtful words made tears flow from his eyes.

"If only the garbage would be friends with me...," he thought. However, the garbage kept making fun of him. Wingtip grew more sad and lonely as the days passed.

One morning, Wingtip heard children playing at the park.

However, the boy's mother was horrified. "Son, don't touch that dirty, old shoe!" she said.

The boy threw Wingtip into the dumpster.

Wingtip landed in a glob of bubblegum on the rim of the dumpster. He was stuck and the garbage made fun of him.

There lay Wingtip—in his new and last home. His hope of finding someone to need him was now gone.

Later that day, Wingtip was startled, by the sound of a garbage truck heading straight towards the dumpster.

The garbage truck brought the dumpster up into the air, and dumped all the garbage into the hopper. All the garbage — except Wingtip, as the bubblegum held him like glue. However, a piece of garbage hit Wingtip with such force that he **flew** into the air ...

bounced off a tree, and slid down the trunk,

landing beside the sidewalk.

Although he was thankful to be out of the dumpster, he still longed for the foot of a new owner. He began to dream of how he could be useful as one shoe, perhaps as a planter or a birdfeeder. "How ridiculous," he sighed.

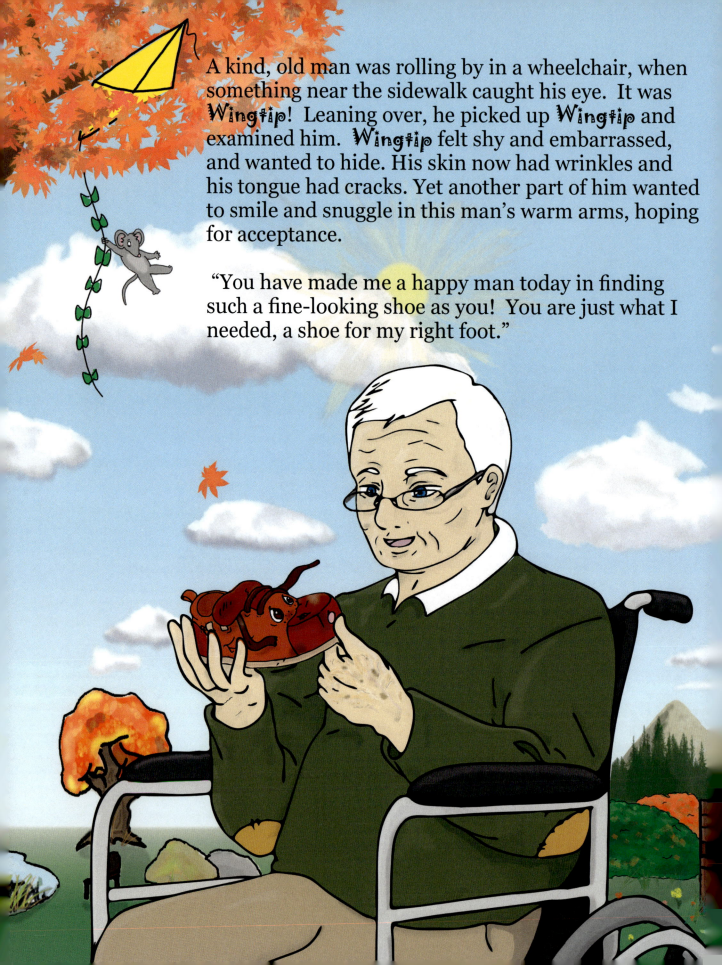

A kind, old man was rolling by in a wheelchair, when something near the sidewalk caught his eye. It was Wingtip! Leaning over, he picked up Wingtip and examined him. Wingtip felt shy and embarrassed, and wanted to hide. His skin now had wrinkles and his tongue had cracks. Yet another part of him wanted to smile and snuggle in this man's warm arms, hoping for acceptance.

"You have made me a happy man today in finding such a fine-looking shoe as you! You are just what I needed, a shoe for my right foot."

The man dusted off Wingtip and smiled at him.
He replaced his old worn-out shoe and put on Wingtip. The fit was
perfect for both of them! The man was grateful for such a prize.

Wingtip could not believe his fortune! "How could anyone
want just one shoe?" he asked himself.
At that moment, Wingtip noticed something . . .

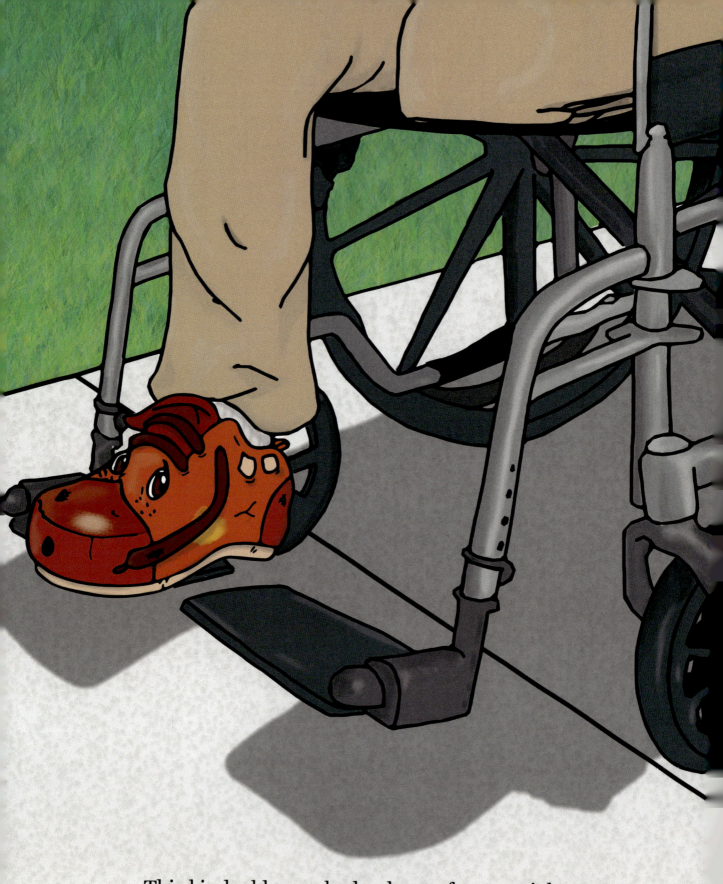

This kind, old man, had only one foot —a right one.

Wingtip again had a home. And the old man and Wingtip rolled happily together for many years.

# GET TO KNOW THE CAST

Wingtip played himself. Born in Boot, Ireland, and speaks with an Irish brogue. He has appeared in men's shoe catalogs, children's picture books, and played in a string quartet. He resides in his closet home with his family of many sizes.

Stitch Instep played the part of Sole. He was the winner in the Wingtip Look-Alike Contest, and won out over other contestants, Velcro and Shoe Horn. He lives in Oxford. He refused any speaking parts, because when he sees a camera, he gets tongue-tied and ends up with knots in his stomach.

Arch Support got the part because he was good-looking and straight-laced, and his feet fit perfectly into Wingtip and Sole. (Wingtip and Sole requested that whoever got the part could not have stinky feet!)

Dog is bilingual, saying "Bow Wow" in Spanish and English. He won an Academy Reward, and given a tattered shoe to gnaw. Dog is still looking for his soul mutt.

All garbage auditioned in "Shoestrings Got Garbage." Those given speaking parts had no prior acting experience. They were naturally sassy and knew how to act like a heel.

Pest was never among the cast, and booted out many times. The author said, "Eyelet him know he'd better toe the mark!" He would sneak in from time-to-time when the illustrator was drawing, hoping to be discovered by a talent scout.
One thing we know about Pest is, his sister dates loafers.

Bird in cage, man in wheelchair, children, mother at park, and all other characters not mentioned on this page were either a, stand-in, walk-in, fly-in, roll-by or shut-in.

Stunt Players were used as garbage when thrown into the dump truck.

*A special thank you to the City of Shoestring for the use of their dumpster and garbage truck while making this picture book.*

*No animal, garbage or shoes were hurt in the making of this book.*

# QUESTIONS
## *A HOME FOR WINGTIP*

1. What was the name of the city where Wingtip lived?

2. Sole had a name that is part of a shoe, where is it on your shoe?

3. When Wingtip saw his owner drive away, how do you think he felt?

4. What are aglets, and how do they help the shoelace?

5. Wingtip had a tongue. Where is the tongue on your shoe?

6. Have you ever had to throw something away that you really liked? How did it make you feel? What was it?

7. Do you show kindness and try to be a friend, when someone feels left out?

8. Wingtip was always looking for a friend. How do you think Wingtip felt when the dog did not want to play with him anymore?

9. The garbage called Wingtip mean names, yet Wingtip did not say mean things back. He showed humbleness and strength. Wingtip did not believe he was worthless or garbage – he knew his worth! Do you believe that everyone has good qualities and look for the good in others? Do you know how important you are?

10. What good qualities do you have? What are you good at doing?

11. Wingtip loved being useful. How does it make you feel when you help others?

12. Sometimes we go through things that seem very bad, but lead to things that are the best for us. What things happened to Wingtip, which seemed bad, but turned out better because of it?

13. When the old man saw Wingtip with his scuffs, wrinkles, and dirt, he still thought of him as a prize. When you see others different or older than you, will you treat them nice and with respect?

14. Would you like to take Wingtip home with you? How could he be useful?

15. Do you have another ending for the story?

16. What are puns? What puns did the author use that had to do with a shoe?

The End

Made in the
USA
Columbia, SC

80756765R10020